Little Billy Bison

Retold by BLAKE HOENA

Illustrated by TIM PALIN

CANTATA
LEARNING

WWW.CANTATALEARNING.COM

CANTATA LEARNING

Published by Cantata Learning
1710 Roe Crest Drive
North Mankato, MN 56003
www.cantatalearning.com

Library of Congress Control Number: 2015932811
Hoena, Blake
    Little Billy Bison / retold by Blake Hoena; Illustrated by Tim Palin
    Series: Tangled Tunes
    Audience: Ages: 3–8; Grades: PreK–3
    Summary: Set to the melody of "The Battle Hymn of the Republic," this delightful
song shows how Little Billy Bison is bothered by a fly, a flea, a grasshopper, and an ant.
    ISBN: 978-1-63290-358-7 (library binding/CD)
    ISBN: 978-1-63290-489-8 (paperback/CD)
    ISBN: 978-1-63290-519-2 (paperback)
    1. Stories in rhymes. 2. American Buffalo (Bison)—fiction.

Book design, Tim Palin Creative
Editorial direction, Flat Sole Studio
Music direction, Elizabeth Draper
Music arranged and produced by Musical Youth Productions

Printed in the United States of America in North Mankato, Minnesota.
122015   0326CGS16

ACCESS THE MUSIC!

SCAN CODE WITH MOBILE APP

CANTATALEARNING.COM

Little Billy **Bison** is **bothered** by a fly, a flea, a grasshopper, and an ant. But Billy is **clever**, and he gets them to go away.

To find out how, turn the page and sing along!

Little Billy Bison had a fly upon his nose.

Little Billy Bison had a fly upon his nose.
So he flicked it, and it flew away!

Clever, clever Billy Bison.

Clever, clever Billy Bison.

Clever, clever Billy Bison.

So he flicked it, and it flew away!

9

Little Billy Bison had a bug upon his ear.
Little Billy Bison had a bug upon his ear.

10

Little Billy Bison had
a bug upon his ear.

So he flapped it,
and it flew away!

11

Clever, clever Billy Bison.
Clever, clever Billy Bison.
Clever, clever Billy Bison.

So he flapped it, and it flew away!

13

Little Billy Bison had a flea upon his tail.

Little Billy Bison had a flea upon his tail.

Little Billy Bison had a flea upon his tail.
So he wiggled it, and it jumped away!

Clever, clever Billy Bison.

Clever, clever Billy Bison.

Clever, clever Billy Bison.

So he wiggled it, and it jumped away!

Little Billy Bison had
an ant upon his hoof.

Little Billy Bison had
an ant upon his hoof.

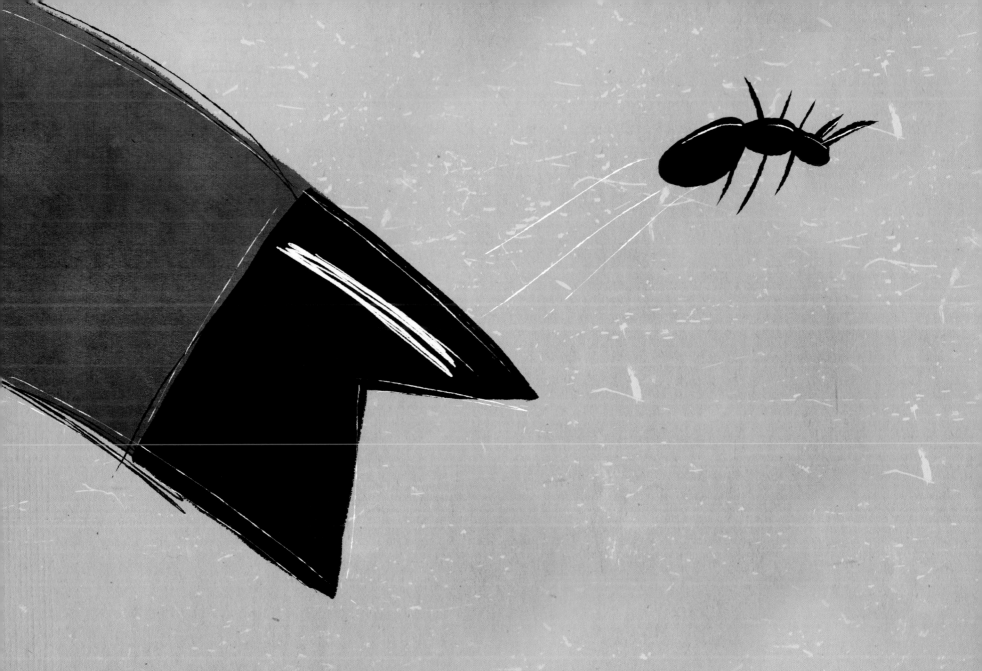

Little Billy Bison had an ant upon his hoof.

So he kicked it, and it flew away!

Clever, clever Billy Bison.
Clever, clever Billy Bison.
Clever, clever Billy Bison.

So he kicked it, and it flew away!

SONG LYRICS
Little Billy Bison

Little Billy Bison had a fly upon his nose.
Little Billy Bison had a fly upon his nose.

Little Billy Bison had a fly upon his nose.
So he flicked it, and it flew away!

Clever, clever Billy Bison.
Clever, clever Billy Bison.
Clever, clever Billy Bison.

So he flicked it, and it flew away!

Little Billy Bison had a bug upon his ear.
Little Billy Bison had a bug upon his ear.

Little Billy Bison had a bug upon his ear.
So he flapped it, and it flew away!

Clever, clever Billy Bison.
Clever, clever Billy Bison.
Clever, clever Billy Bison.

So he flapped it, and it flew away!

Little Billy Bison had a flea upon his tail.
Little Billy Bison had a flea upon his tail.

Little Billy Bison had a flea upon his tail.
So he wiggled it, and it jumped away!

Clever, clever Billy Bison.
Clever, clever Billy Bison.
Clever, clever Billy Bison.

So he wiggled it, and it jumped away!

Little Billy Bison had an ant upon his hoof.
Little Billy Bison had an ant upon his hoof.

Little Billy Bison had an ant upon his hoof.
So he kicked it, and it flew away!

Clever, clever Billy Bison.
Clever, clever Billy Bison.
Clever, clever Billy Bison.

So he kicked it, and it flew away!